This book belongs to:

Li'l Miss Fuss Budget

By Kate Allen

Illustrated by Jessica Blanset

The Kumquat Press

Lauren, Ted, Wilma, Tim, Marie, Jessica, Kristin, Ingrid, Ron, Fiona, Ken, Michael, Bob, and Reed.

Summary: A brother and sister's hilarious look at growing up.

Manufactured in Hong Kong

To my little Miss Fuss Budget, Lauren

and

my brother, Jim

Kate

To my little Miss Fuss Budget twins,

Kristin and Ingrid

Jessica

Li'l Miss Fuss Budget lives at our house.
Every morning she gets up and fusses about.

Grandma thinks she's a bit haughty.
Mom says "No, she's just naughty."

Grandpa believes it's just a bout.
Not me — I say "Get out!!!"

On Monday she sits in the middle of the floor
and declares her clothes are such a bore.

On Tuesday she yells "Breakfast stinks!"
and throws it in the kitchen sink.

On Wednesday she makes quite a fuss.
She won't even ride the bus.

On Thursday what a horrible bear.
  She refuses to brush her teeth and hair.

On Friday Dad says "That's it!"
He gives time-out for sis to sit.

On Saturday she's still pouting
and there's an awful lot of shouting.

On Sunday she puts on her fancy dress
and tries to give us all some rest.

Mom and Dad can't wait till the day
when Li'l Miss Fuss Budget's phase goes away.

But I confess I had my own stage.
And I know it's just my sister's age.

I'll keep her forever

and ever—

I guess.

For after all— she is the BEST!!!

KATE ALLEN, AUTHOR

Born in a small town in Missouri, Kate comes from several generations of fussy fuss budgets. Her Texan husband, her 11-year-old daughter, and her seven dogs often hide from Kate when she wants to read them her story '...just one more time.' Her humor and love of children and animals are evident throughout her books. She is the author of *The Legend of the Whistle Pig Wrangler* and *The Lizard Who Followed Me Home* and is working on several other children's books. Kate lives on a ranch in Southern California with her husband, daughter, and a large family of adored pets.

JESSICA BLANSET, ILLUSTRATOR

Born in a small town in Missouri, Jessica is one of three fuss budget sisters. Raising 12-year-old twins provides her with much inspiration for her cartoons and illustrations. Jessica's husband Ron sums up her humorous view of life best. 'Tess, you see life as one big cartoon.' Her illustrations appear in national advertising campaigns and magazines. Currently producing a series of dog cartoons, Jessica lives in Chicago with Ron, Ingrid, Kristin, their dog, George, and cat, Tomasina.

KATE'S DOG

Woody was thrilled to be the inspiration for Fuss Budget's dog. At age 2, he enjoys basketball, football, and catching a pop fly. He loves to sign autographs and is always up for a good wrestling match.

JESSICA'S DOG

George was a natural model for Fuss Budget's dog and has a great future in dog cartoons — if he can stop eating the letters that fall through the mail slot. His favorite pastime is lying around and playing with the twins.